JOHNNY'S TRAIL

Anne Eliot Crompton

SWEDENBORG FOUNDATION
NEW YORK

First Printing 1986

ISBN 0-87785-131-X
Library of Congress Catalog Card Number 86-60054

All Rights Reserved
Copyright © Swedenborg Foundation 1986

Cover and book design by Nancy Crompton

Swedenborg Foundation, Inc.
139 East 23rd Street
New York, New York 10010

Manufactured in the United States of America

AUTHOR'S NOTE

This story is almost true. Johnny really lived in Ohio in 1812, and his legend says he did most of the things mentioned in this book.

The other people in the story are fictional characters, but they are very like the folk Johnny really knew. Because their talk is somewhat different from ours, there is a glossary of words and phrases at the back of this book.

Brief biographies of Johnny (John Chapman) and his inspiration, Emanuel Swedenborg, can also be found at the back of this book.

Chapter 1.

MY NAME IS PERSIS. I am fourteen.

I crouch among huge sycamore roots, hugging my knees. My skirt is torn and dirty. My ankle is tied tightly with a rawhide thong. The other end of the thong attaches to a sapling. I can't untie the knot on my ankle. I could untie the sapling end, but the Painted Men would notice. I doubt what would happen then.

The Painted Men wear breech clouts and moccasins, feathers, and black and red paint. New scalps dangle from their belts. They bristle with weapons, bows and guns and knives. They jabber softly to each other in wild, strange words. Yellow sunlight falls on them through high, shifting leaves. Yellow leaves drop in my lap. I shiver. The air is cool, and I feel sick.

One Painted Man owns me. He keeps a sharp eye on me and on the rawhide thong. Just now he gave me a handful of parched corn, but I couldn't eat it. I've got it in my fist.

Owner looks over at me now, and past me. His black eyes widen a trace. He points with his chin. The other Painted Men look where he points. Eagle Feather, in charge, heists his rifle. I look round. Yonder is a thicket of little shaky alders. A twig snaps. A man comes sidling out of the alders, hands high, smiling. Lo, a white man.

He is small and thin, with straight dark hair and a sparse black beard. He wears—fact!—a coffee sack with arm and neck holes, and a tin mush pot on his head. Also a leather bag and a belt with dangling pouches. He carries no gun, only a hunting knife and a walking stick. His feet are bare.

The Painted Men murmur. Owner touches his head, the others nod. I agree. White man is crazy.

He keeps coming, slowly, hands up. Eagle Feather lowers his gun. Crazy White Man walks right up to him, says "Hey!" They hunker down, nose to nose. The Painted Men close in around them. I can't see much from here.

Now I might try to untie the knot from the sapling and slink off in the woods. But where to? I don't know where I am.

Crazy and Eagle Feather talk some while. Pipes appear and the air gets smoky. At last they stand up. Crazy takes a little box out of a pouch and shakes into Owner's hands. Owner stows it away in his own pouch. They come over to me. The other Painted Men watch. Owner starts to untie the thong from my ankle, but he can't. He's obliged to cut it off with a knife. Crazy leans and takes my hand and pulls me upright. My foot is numb, I can't stand on it. But Crazy leads me firmly away. I have to rabbit-hop after him. The Painted Men laugh. Crazy tramps through the alders like they aren't even there. They catch my hair, my skirt, reach for my eyes. I have to hop right smart, he won't slow down.

Beyond the alders Crazy commences to run. I can either fall down or run too, so I run. My foot screams and screams but I run, and after a bit I'm able, and Crazy lets go my hand. He runs faster, and I run after his disappearing back, because I don't know what else to do. There's only autumn-yellow woods everywhere, and the Painted Men behind us. I dassn't lose sight of Crazy. He's all I know.

He slows to a fast walk. We go on for a while and a while. The same leaning ash tree keeps turning up. I reckon we're backtracking and circling to confuse our track. Maybe Crazy isn't stupid.

He stops. I come up panting, and lo, there's a spring of clear water at his feet. I drop on my knees, cup my hands and drink forever. Crazy drinks leaning over the spring, scooping water with one hand. Then he fills a pouch with water. He moves into a thicket and beckons me. I follow. We sit down well into the thicket, and Crazy pulls branches in front to hide us. We turn to each other.

His eyes are dark blue, kind, almost sweet. I open my fist and show him my parched corn, still there. He takes a pinch, I take a pinch. We polish it off.

Crazy says softly, "One time I was running from those fellows, those Wyandots. Not the same ones. Same tribe. Couldn't shake them. Had to walk into a pondful of cat-tails and lie down amongst.

"The Wyandots came up, splashed around searching. One of them darn near stepped on me. But I was well down in the water by then, breathing through a straw. When they went off I didn't dare come up. Had a nice long nap down there in the reeds. My name's Johnny. What's yours?"

"Persis."

Johnny smiles. "Persis is my favorite girl's name. What's the other name goes with it?"

"Don't know."

He twitches his nose. Johnny's nose turns up so far it draws up his lip. One yellow tooth shows all the time. "Who are your folks?"

"Don't know."

"Where were you when the Wyandots caught you?"

"Don't know."

"Hah. I see." Johnny looks me over like I'm a strange dog he might want to pet. "Well," he says, "You're a good sturdy girl, Persis. You can run, 'spite of being chunky. And good looking, with your yellow hair." His finger brushes my long scraggled braid. "That's how I noticed you were white. Otherwise, I'd just have sneaked on by those Wyandots. They are unfriendly folk, not that you can blame them. Well, I bet you've got folks and a home that you'll remember bye and bye."

"Where are we, Johnny?"

"In the woods," says he, and his blue eyes twinkle. He adds, "Between Lake Erie and Mansfield, Ohio. Folks sent me to scout these trails, see what the British and Wyandots are up to. This is a year of war, and rumors of war."

"What year is it?"

"Why, the year of the Lord, eighteen hundred and twelve." Johnny looks sharp at me. He thinks I'm funning.

"I really don't know nothing." It's true. There's a fog in my head.

Johnny says, "I believe you, Persis. Now be quiet. Listen to the woods."

We listen. Wind sighs, leaves rustle and fall. Wings flap. Silence.

"Reckon they didn't follow, or we shook them. We'd best be off. Got a power of ground to cover by night."

He's up and away, swinging his walking stick.

I trot behind, and pretty soon I'm panting. Johnny keeps up a steady pace through thicket and briar and ropes of fox-grape, till we hit a trail. Hah! Now, I think, travel will be easier. But Johnny just goes faster. I'm running again. His coffee-sack back disappears behind leaves, around bends, and I dassn't lose him! When he stops I run into him.

Chapter 2.

IN FRONT IS A PIT, dug to twice Johnny's height. Johnny is a small man; make that two and a half times his height. At the bottom something snarls and groans. Teeth snap and gnash. Eyes glare, yellow as autumn leaves. It turns and turns about in the depth of the pit, dark fur, clashing teeth. It jumps up on hind legs to snap at Johnny's bare toes. He takes a step backward.

I skip way back. "Johnny," say I, voice shaking, "That's a wolf, there."

"You're right," says he.

"Somebody trapped it."

"Aye."

"But we can walk around."

Johnny studies the pit. He says, "A mountain cat, now, he could claw his way out." He wanders off a bit, studying. "Wolf might never get out of there."

"Fine. Let's go." Get away before it finds a way out.

Johnny finds what he's been studying for. With his two bare hands he knocks a rotten branch off an oak tree and drags it to the pit. "Wolf," he says, "Stand aside." And he thrusts the branch down slantwise into the pit.

I run for the oak. Halfway up I twist around to see what's happened to Johnny. Or maybe I should still call him just Crazy.

He's still standing there. The awesome snapping and snarling has stopped, the pit is silent. I can see the branch sticking up. It jiggles and slides around. The wolf must be climbing it. "That's the way," says Crazy. The wolf's head rises out of the pit. It glares at Crazy.

Crazy backs off a way.

I yell, "Johnny, up here!" But he doesn't look round.

The wolf scrambles out of the pit.

It's big, dark brown and gray. I hold my breath and wait for it to tear Johnny in shreds.

"There now," he says, peaceably.

The wolf gives him a long look. Slowly, it walks around the pit. It stops and looks down into the pit and snarls.

It walks away. Red and yellow leaves swing to behind it, like curtains. It's gone.

Crazy calls, "Persis?"

I climb down the oak. I went up without knowing. Down is harder. I say, "Mister, you're crazy."

Johnny twitches his nose at me. "Folks do say that. Well, let us be going."

And we're off.

All day Johnny strides silently. Rarely he brushes a branch or breaks a twig. There's something Indian about Johnny. I feel he knows everything around us, what we see and what's beyond. Like he's got six senses. At one point he stops, wheels, looks past me. I turn. And there, at the bend in the trail, stands Wolf.

I breathe, "It's following you!"

"Aye," says Johnny. He wheels about and strides on.

I run after. I keep glancing over my shoulder, though, and right soon I'm sure Wolf is after us. Sometimes it's a flick of a shadow just disappearing into brush. Sometimes it stands plain to see, watching us, twitching its ears. It's waiting for me to fall behind, like a feeble fawn behind a fast doe. It hears me panting.

All day I run after Johnny's disappearing back. The sun is low when at last he stops again. He points with his little black beard, dead ahead.

The trail leads out across a clearing. The clearing is dim, kind of cloudy. And now I smell the cloud. It's smoke. In the middle of the clearing stand a few burned black posts, and in the midst a pile of black rubble that used to be a cabin.

Johnny and I teeter like deer on the edge of the clearing. Our eyes dart hither and yon. Our ears practically wiggle, we listen so hard. Johnny wrinkles his nose and sniffs. There's no sound but a steady rustle of falling leaves. No smell but smoke. Nothing moves. After a while Johnny says, very soft, "Wyandot. Gone, now. You stay here, just in case." He advances into the clearing.

I wait for an arrow to hiss or a gun to boom. Johnny walks on to the burned cabin.

Behind me, something watches.

I turn. Wolf sits not ten paces away. Its ears twitch, its yellow eyes glow. I run out yonder after Johnny.

He's searching around in the ashes. I wait outside. Wolf does not follow. It's probably skulking around the clearing.

Johnny says, "Nothing in here. Likely the Wyandots caught them."

"Or they escaped."

"Oh. Aye." But Johnny's voice says No.

Something occurs to me. I walk around the outside toward the setting sun. Here is the well, a stone-lined hole by what was the kitchen door. I know it by the long flat beam where you sit to shell peas or husk corn. Something else occurs to me. I wander farther.

Here is the garden, what's left of it. I walk among dry, yellow squash vines. Beans climb leaning bare cornstalks. I pull handfuls of beans and hold them in my skirt. Some I shell and eat.

Johnny comes up and opens a pouch. We stuff it full of beans. "That's well thought," says he. "Now let's be gone from here."

Just inside the woods we come upon a wooden cross, burned with letters. "Grave marker," says Johnny. "It may tell us who lived here." He studies it. I wait, shifting my aching feet. My moccasins are walked to ribbons; tomorrow I'll be barefoot.

"No name," says Johnny. "Nice inscription."

"Aye. It's prettily done."

"I mean, what it says."

"What's it say?"

"You can't read?"

"Why, no." Who can?

Johnny can. He reads aloud from the cross.

" 'Thirteen years I was a daughter, Two years I was a wife, One year I was a mother, The next year took my life.' "

The fog in my head shifts and rolls. I say, "That reminds me of . . . something."

"You seen this grave before, Persis?"

"I . . . seem to think so."

"Well. It will all come back to you, once you're safe and rested." Johnny doffs his mushpot hat to the cross with an odd, gracious manner, and turns away.

I doubt I can ever find these trails again even if it does "all come back." The last light fades. The woods are gray and turning black. Johnny keeps glancing behind us. Maybe he's wondering if we really did shake the Wyandots this morning. I look back myself. The trail behind is a faint blur of gray on black. Something moves there.

"Johnny, someone's following!"

"Wolf," he reassures me. "Just Wolf, that's all."

Just Wolf, that's all! Lo, I'm running in the dark, legs giving out, moccasins wore out, and there's a wolf on my trail! And Johnny says, "That's all!"

I pant, "Listen, Johnny. I can't go any more."

As if to prove it, I catch a toe on a root and sprawl flat. "Johnny!" I bawl. I can just see Johnny vanishing around a bush, and Wolf right on my heels!

Johnny turns back and picks me up. "By jingo," he says cheerfully, "You're right wore out. I forgot you probably don't hike like I do."

Agreeing, I catch my breath.

"We'll sleep aloft," he decides. "Always wise in unknown territory."

"Aloft?"

"In a tree. In this one here. Plenty of sturdy branches. You got business to do, you go thataway. I'll go thisaway for the same purpose."

Johnny vanishes. Not hard to do in this black-as-Egypt night. I find my way into a thicket and do business. But coming out I can't find Johnny or his tree. Something patters nearby. Something goes bump. Wolf can't be far off. I yell, "Johnny!"

A screech owl answers.

"JOHNNY!"

The screech owl quavers reproachfully. Hah! It's Johnny. Indians signal like that, and so does he. I make toward it. In a moment my hand is on the rough bark of the tree.

"Up you go, Percy." Johnny hoists me up the trunk. By the bark and the lay of the branches I reckon it's a mighty maple. Johnny swarms up and pulls me into a safe, wide crotch. Here we nestle. Leaves whisper and rustle around, above and below. Up here we must be safe. I breathe free, for the first time all day.

I feel Johnny dealing with his knapsack. He finds my hand, opens it, presses corn into it. Also beans. We eat in silence, a handful of parched corn, a handful of beans. "Don't drop the shells," he warns. "Our Wyandot friends might notice." Last, we share the water he saved at the spring.

My feet are numb. My back fits itself snug against the maple trunk and relaxes. I'm nearly asleep when Johnny murmurs, "I don't know these parts."

I jerk awake.

"I know the trails from Marietta and Newark to Mansfield, and every cabin on them. I've peddled my trees to every settler moved into that territory. But up here I'm a stranger and a sojourner. A scout. Know where I was last week?"

"No." I don't where *I* was last week.

"Last week I was running from one cabin to the next. As I came to each one I called out, 'The spirit of the Lord is upon me, and He hath anointed me to blow the trumpet in the wilderness, and sound the alarm in the forest; for behold, the tribes of the heathen are round about your doors, and a devouring flame followeth after them!' I ran near thirty miles one night."

Sleepy, foggy and fuddled, I yet doubt this story. "Did you really say all that at every cabin?"

"Well, no, not exactly. That's what I meant to say. But often enough I'd be out of breath and just yell, 'Flee for your lives! The British and Indians are coming upon you, and destruction followeth in their footsteps!' "

"And did it?"

"Aye, destruction followed for sure. Several neighbors killed and their cabins burned, like the one we found today. Now, if that was down Mansfield way, I'd know who it was. I know everyone. But I didn't know there was a cabin there at all, never mind who lived there."

Johnny is silent a bit, and I nod off again. His next murmur wakes me like a shot. "Do you remember, Percy?"

"I don't remember nothing."

"Thought it might have come to you out of the dark. You seemed to know that grave."

"Aye, Well, I had a . . . feeling." I say it mostly to please him, and then I know it's true. I really do have a feeling. "Maybe I lived there once."

"Those were your folks, Percy?" How gently he whispers!

"No, not my folks. I just lived there. Worked there."

"Aye. You knew about the garden, and the beans."

"Sort of."

"It will come back," he says firmly. " 'The interior memory vastly excels the exterior.' " Whatever that means. I'm too sleepy to ask.

"Percy, do you know anything at all about your own folks?"

"Aye." I hear myself say it. The words keep coming. "I remember my Mama dying."

A clear picture forms in my foggy mind. Mama lies under a patchwork beside a hearth. In the firelight her hair shines gold, all over the pillow. Her face is turned away from me, toward the fire. She breathes hard.

A man grabs me up in his arms. I must be quite small, six or seven. I struggle, but he carries me away with no trouble, out the door, into a snowstorm. I hear myself say sadly, "Mama's dead."

Johnny says, "So is mine. Died when I was little. It's rough for us, Percy, but it's fine for them. Our mothers are angels in Heaven, now."

"Hah! I'll believe in angels when I see one."

"All right," says Johnny. "I will show you one."

"You will?"

"Maybe tomorrow. Then you'll believe?"

"Show me an angel, I'll believe it."

"Done!"

How can a grown man talk this way?

Johnny waits till I'm nodding asleep. Then he says, "One spring I canoed down the Allegheny for supplies. The ice was running. I was hard put to it to keep the canoe upright, and I was tiring." Johnny, tiring? "So I heisted the canoe up on a block of ice floating downstream. I curled up and slept, there in the canoe, which canoe rested on the ice, which ice rushed downstream. When I woke up I was a hundred miles farther than I meant to go." He sighs happily, remembering that good time. "Sleep well, Percy, and fear not. For 'The Lord guards man with most especial care during his sleep.'"

I suspicion Johnny's legs are stronger than his brain.

Chapter 3.

MY NAME IS PERSIS. I am fourteen.

Dawn creeps misty-yellow through the woods. Leaves drop around us. What wakes me is the sound of baying hounds, coming fast. Could the Wyandots be hunting us with hounds?

No. The sound is above us, sweeping over us. Through a window of dropped leaves I see a V of wild geese stream south across the sky.

What am I doing here? And where is here?

I'm waking up in a maple crotch, cramped, numb, and very hungry. I have business to do down below. I lean out a bit, look down—and draw back.

At the foot of the maple, cushioned in rusty ferns, sits Wolf. It yawns up at me. Its teeth are long and yellow.

I doubt I ever woke up in a tree before, certainly

not with a wolf under it! I hope I never woke up scrunched beside a strange man, either. But here is Johnny, snoring beside me.

He's all wound up with his bare feet on one great limb and his back on another. His mushpot hat tilts to shield him from the growing light. Even curled and coiled like this he seems comfortable. Strong. By jingo, look at those muscles like thongs! He's a physical marvel, a little lean man with the strength of an ox. Mentally, he may be lacking.

And lo, here I am alone with him in a maple crotch in an autumn wood, with a wolf licking its chops every time I look down.

Where was I yesterday? Who am I, and who was I yesterday?

My name is Persis. I am fourteen.

I was with the Wyandots, tied to a sapling. Earlier, they tied my hands. Earlier . . . nothing. Fog. However I arrived there, I was with the Wyandots tied to a sapling, and this Johnny came along and bought me. Why?

He didn't need to bother with me. He's scouting for his neighbors, fretted about Indians and British. He didn't need to buy me and share his rations with me. He didn't need to help Wolf out of the pit, either, and I wish he hadn't!

Hah! I remember the pit, and the burned cabins, and the grave, and the garden with beans.

I'm going to have to trust Johnny. I have no

choice. It's Johnny for me, or else it's Wolf and the Wyandots. Look how he sleeps, curled a little below me. So an enemy climbing would get to him first. I really have to get down out of this tree.
Wolf stretches and looks up at me hungrily.
I lift the mushpot off Johnny's face. His eyes flash open. No mumbling, no misty groping. Johnny is wide awake. He smiles at me sweetly. He says, "This is the day that the Lord has made. Let us be glad and rejoice in it."
First thing he does, he pulls a small snuffbox out of a pouch and opens it. Eagerly he lifts it to his nose, sniffs. A look of deep disappointment crosses his face. "Hah," he says. "I forgot." And closes the snuffbox and stashes it away.
"Johnny," say I, "I have to get down."
"Go ahead, Percy."
"Look yonder." I point. Wolf grins and swings his tail a little, like a dog.
Johnny laughs. "Don't fret about Wolf! He just wants to be our friend."
"Your friend, maybe. Not mine."
"Well," says Johnny, "If you feel that way, that's how he feels, too. I'll come down."
He stretches, breathes deep, and swings down beside Wolf. Wolf backs off a bit, lowers his head, bares his teeth. Johnny pays no attention. "Come on down now," he tells me, and holds up his arms. I scramble down into them, and he lifts me the

rest of the way. Quickly I step to the far side of him, away from Wolf.

"Let's go break our fast," says Johnny. "Precious little rations left here." He pats his pouches. "Wolf and I'll go north, you go south. We'll meet back here."

"What should I look for?"

"What the Lord provides. Late berries, nuts. Once I lived a winter on beechnuts."

I dassn't go far. Just turn around in the woods and you can get lost. One eye on the red glow of maple leaves, I forage cautiously. Mushrooms are everywhere, bright and spotty amongst fallen leaves. Some you can relish, some you can endure, some kill you dead. And I doubt which are which.

I'm stiff from sleeping in the tree, and running all yesterday. I'm famished, thirsty and fretted, mistaking every pattering leaf for Wolf's footfall.

Arriving back at the maple with a skirtful of groundnuts, I'm glad to find Johnny there with wild greens. We eat quickly, standing. Johnny shares out his last water, takes up his walking stick, and sets off. I trot after him. Glancing back I see no Wolf. But I doubt that means it has deserted Johnny.

Now the sun is high, the woods are golden. We trot through ferns, over brown pine needles, between fire-red sumacs. I'm getting into the swing of this.

The sun is higher when Johnny stops. There is

no spring, nothing to forage. He just stops in the middle of the trail, listening.

It's a crash, step, thud, behind that willow thicket. I seem to hear teeth snapping, but maybe that's just my fretfulness. Something runs, stops, wheels, and runs toward us. Willows crack and break.

"Johnny..."

"Quiet."

I am quiet.

It's large and white. Whiteness moves fast through the willows. It snorts like...

A big white head pokes out of the nearest thicket. It regards us mournfully.

I sigh with huge relief. "It's just a horse!"

The face is sad-eyed, ridged with age. The horse shakes its burr-tangled mane and snorts again. Behind it, teeth definitely snap. It plods into the open.

It's a tall, ancient plowhorse, rib-thin and swaybacked. As Wolf lopes out of the willows, it gathers what looks like its last strength to kick. Wolf springs lightly aside and sits down, grinning.

Johnny tells the horse, "Easy, old fellow." He makes slowly toward it. It backs off suspiciously, till he lays a calming hand on its neck.

To Wolf he says, "Thank you for the good dinner."

"Dinner?"

"Wolf expects us to eat this old codger."

By all means! I'm hungry enough to eat a horse by myself!

"Some farmer turned him loose to forage," Johnny goes on, patting the horse's nose. "Didn't want to feed him any more. He's about wore out."

The mist in my head lifts like a curtain. I see a tall, spare man driving a brown horse into winter woods. He swings a chain and yells, and the horse keeps trying to circle back to its warm barn. I say aloud, "Mr. Wheeler!"

"What?"

"Mr. Wheeler drove his old horse away like that."

"He a relation of yours?"

"No. No . . . I worked for him."

"He live at that burned cabin we found?"

"I . . . don't know."

"Well, farmers do drive out old horses. I find them most autumns, starved like this one. He'll never make the winter on his own. We'll take him along with us. Maybe find him a home." Like me. Johnny's finding me a home, too.

Wolf and I watch Johnny make a collar of sorts from foxgrape and slip it over the horse's stringy neck. "He'll need a name," he murmurs. "Pegasus, that suits him. Peg for short."

"That's a strange name."

"Pegasus was a winged horse in an old pagan tale. Carried a hero through the sky." A far cry from this ancient wreck! Johnny fastens the vine collar and hands me the long lead. "You lead him, Percy."

"Lead him!"

"Aye. Can't ride him, you know. Sway-back'll never hold up. 'Specially with you so chunky."

I glance down at myself. I don't feel chunky. Right now I feel downright thin.

Johnny wrinkles his nose. "Just funning you. Wolf, don't look crestfallen. We're grateful to you, even if we don't dine on Peg."

We're off again, Johnny first, then me leading Peg. He hangs back on the vine lead. His hoofs pound tiredly at my heels.

Chapter 4.

AT HIGH NOON all the shifting, shaking, falling leaves gleam like fool's gold. Peg's hoofbeats thud heavy behind me, a little slower all the time. Peg is wearing down, and so am I. Wolf has vanished in the woods. Johnny says it likes to circle us, starting up game and scouting. It would warn us of Indians, he says. I doubt.

Johnny marches ahead, walking stick swinging. He takes a log in his stride. On the other side a long thick vine whips up as high as his waist.

Johnny jumps ten feet high.

Peg snorts and jerks the lead out of my hand.

A thick stick lies at my feet. I grab it up and charge to flatten that serpent. Stick high, I leap the log. Yonder goes the serpent, gliding away like a shadow into orange ferns, rattling as it writhes.

"Johnny!" I scream. "Did it bite?"

"No. No, he missed." Johnny stands gasping. His blue eyes glaze. I doubt the snake may have bit him. He sways.

"Come, sit down." I take his arm, guide him to sit down on the log. First I look under it. There might be another rattler.

I sit down with Johnny, hand on his arm. Fact, I'm shaking. I drop the stick. It's the same color as the snake. Might easily have been a snake, and me grabbing it by the tail! I shudder.

We sit silent till we quit shaking. The noon sun comforts us, shimmering warm between leaves. After a bit Johnny feels out his snuffbox, opens it, leans to it. It's empty. "Hah," he says faintly. "I forgot again." He looks around as if he's just waking up. "Peg's run off. Won't go far."

"Not he!"

"Persis, I want to thank you for coming up so brave and prompt. I appreciate that mightily."

I look down in my torn, dirty lap and blush.

Come to think, it was a darnfool thing to do! The rattler could have bit us both. What was I thinking of?

Fact, I need Johnny. Without him I would never get out of these woods. Or find out who I am. That's why I did it.

Another fact. I like Johnny. He's crazy, but he's good.

Right now his craziness shows. "I'm glad you

didn't hurt him, though. There he lay, basking in the sun, like we are now. And I come along and step on him. Poor fellow, he was upset."

I can only stare.

"I'm right grateful for your help, Percy, and right glad you did no harm. Never hurt a living creature if you can help."

I find my tongue. "A dead snake's a good snake." That's what Mr. Wheeler would say. Did say.

Johnny shakes his head. It's bare. His mushpot must have flown off when he jumped. His dark hair is thinning on top. Wonder how old he is?

" 'All things in the world,' " he declares, " 'Exist from a Divine origin. All God's creatures have spiritual correspondences and uses.' " Johnny has a special lofty tone of voice for such declarations. I think he's talking someone else's words, probably Bible. " 'Nothing natural can exist without something spiritual corresponding to it,' " he goes on. " 'It is plain that as each and all things in the world have come forth from the Divine, they continue to come forth from the Divine.' " In his own voice he adds, "The Lord made that rattler sure as He made you and me, and for a reason." And, returning to his grand tone, " 'The whole Heaven is full of uses, so that it ought to be called the Kingdom of Uses.' And so is this world where we're sitting right now. Every creature has its uses."

By jingo, it's good to sit still and hear Johnny talk! My aching muscles love it. Best thing I can do is keep him talking. When he preaches he sits still. I ask, "What about us people, Johnny? Do we have uses, too?"

Very earnestly he answers, "For sure! Each person has his own use, given him by the Lord."

"How about you?" I tease. "What use in the world are you, Johnny?"

He turns and faces me square, astonished that I don't know. "Why, I'm an orchardman! I plant apple trees."

"Where?"

"Why, all over the Territory! Wherever I see settlers will come, I come there first and plant orchards. Then when they come I've got seedlings to sell. Ain't nothing in this world more useful! Talk about uses. You try doing without apples! Where'd you get sauces and butters, cider and jack, vinegar for pickles and mincemeat? Tell me that!"

I shrug helplessly.

"And I have another use as well," Johnny adds triumphantly. "Planting my orchards, I stop at cabins and camps and Indian towns, and everywhere I stop I bring them the Good News Right Straight From Heaven. Look here, Percy."

He swings his leather bag around and lifts from it a great heavy Bible, very much used. I had no notion he carried such weight around! "Study on that." He opens it on my lap.

"I can't read."

"Oh, aye. I forgot." He takes the Bible back. "But

you have other gifts and uses. I'll never forget how you ran up when you thought I was bit by that rattler. Most young'uns would have run the other way, like Peg." That reminds him of where we are, and why. My heart sinks as he jumps up. "We've a power of a way to go, and the sun high!"

Wolf rises from a hidden fern bed. We never saw it sneak back to us; it just drifted in and lay down while we talked. It shakes and yawns now like a dog. The long teeth snap shut and it looks to Johnny as if to ask, "Where to now?" I'm not much afraid of it now. It knows I belong to Johnny.

"My hat," says Johnny, searching. "Where'd my hat go . . . Percy, go round up Peg while I find my hat."

I travel carefully, and step over no logs without looking behind them! But Peg's trail of broken twig and trampled fern is plain. Lo, there he moves like a white cloud beyond red sumacs. I trot up and catch his trailing vine lead. He jerks up his head and snorts, but I speak to him like Johnny would. "It's just me, Peg, just old Persis here." I lay my hand softly on the tough old neck and pat. Peg's suspicious left eye rolls at me. The other is milky, maybe blind.

He gentles and snuffs my arm. His soft nose moves over my shoulder, he blows warm breath down my back. "Peg," I tell him, "I wish you really were a winged horse and could carry us through the sky!" Over serpents and wolves and brambles and bears and Indians and poison ivy, to wherever it is we're going.

Peg snuffles gently. He wishes so, too.

Chapter 5.

THE FIRST WARNING is a smell.

It comes drifting through the leaves, faint at first, then strong enough to notice. It's smoke.

Johnny pauses, much to my and Peg's delight. I lean against a tree. Peg blows, shifts his weight and lets his head sink.

"Smoke," Johnny mutters. "The Lord be thanked!" He wiggles his nose and grins. "I nearly forgot! This is still north of my trail, but we're getting toward Civilization. That's the Partridge homestead we smell."

I ask hopefully, "Will we stop?" Hoping and yet fearing. It would be great to sleep indoors and eat real food! And yet . . . I doubt who I am, where I belong. What may these Partridges be like? What may they think of me?

"Aye, we'll stop. I must warn them about the Wyandots."

"Will you call out, 'The spirit of the Lord is upon me and He has sent me . . .'"

"No, no. Panic is uncalled for. They need merely be watchful."

Johnny advances. I cluck to Peg and follow. Glancing back, I notice Wolf stopped back at the last bend in the trail. Nose and tail high, it sniffs the smoke.

The woods open out. Yonder are patches of girdled, dying trees and burned clearings. From one clearing a great voice bellows. I jump. A brown ox stands foursquare, watching us from under shining horns.

Now we hear a steady ringing sound ahead. Says Johnny, "Jeremiah Partridge is cutting winter wood." He breaks into an eager trot. So do I and Peg, though my feet are about falling off.

I glance over my shoulder. No Wolf trots after us. It doubts the Civilization ahead, as I do myself. I'm torn between hope and fret. Part of me would like to slink off and hide, like Wolf.

A black and white sow with piglets roots under a beech tree. Partridges will have winter meat, too! A hen cackles under a blueberry bush. We come into a wide open space.

A goodly cabin squats in the middle, defended by a split rail fence. Smoke dawdles up from the sod chimney. Two axes ring together out of sight, behind the cabin.

In the dooryard an ancient, bonneted Grannie bends over a huge iron kettle. Steadily smoking her pipe, she pole-stirs something in the kettle. Now I see it's washing. A little small girl takes the clothes Grannie lifts out on her pole and skips away to hang them on the fence. Pert, red pigtails bounce as she skips. By the door a big girl, my size, pounds corn in a mortar. Her braid and dress are brown, her feet are bare. Right off at first sight I know who she is. She's the slavey. Like me. I was the Wheeler slavey, she's the Partridge slavey. I feel a bit better now about walking out there. Yonder is someone like me.

Johnny strides out. The people don't notice, but three great hounds leap up by the fence and bound toward us baying. "Hallo the house!" shouts Johnny.

The little girl and the slavey look up. Grannie smokes and stirs. Probably deaf.

The little girl dashes through the open gate. She swoops to Johnny, arms wide, like a swallow. He drops his walking stick and opens his arms. As the hounds come swarming and roaring around Peg and me, the little girl hurls herself into Johnny's arms. "Emmy!" He coos, heisting her. "How's my Emmy this fine fall day?"

I doubt I care for this brat! She wraps her little arms around Johnny's neck and smiles over his shoulder, right pleased with herself. See, says her smile, I'm the favorite! If Emmy was older, I reckon I'd hate her.

Peg seems accustomed to dogs, yet he stamps uneasily as these hounds leap about us. One is black, two brown and white. All are lean and strong and not over-friendly. I speak to them and they quiet a bit. Still they circle us, barking in turn.

Slavey shades her eyes with her hand to see us better. Now she turns and walks quickly away behind the cabin. One ax stops ringing.

Johnny bends, Emmy in one arm, picks up his stick and proceeds into the yard. One by one, the hounds run to him. When he speaks, they droop their ears and whine. They know him well. They would like to jump into his arms like Emmy.

Peg picks up his pace. He knows Civilization when he sees it. Maybe he hopes for corn. So do I.

Grannie looks up from her kettle. The pipe almost falls out of her smile. "Why!" she calls clearly, "God bless you, Appleseed John! Lovely are the feet!"

By jingo, the unloveliest feet in the world must be Johnny's bare ones, all scratched and hard as horn! But from somewhere a line comes into my head, 'Lovely on the mountains are the feet of those who bring good tidings.' Must be Bible. Grannie knows Johnny and his Good News from Heaven. Everyone knows my Johnny!

A man comes around the cabin grinning, friendly hand held out. Mr. Partridge is short, stout, hard and bald. The top of his head is white, where the cap usually rests. Other than that, he's tanned deep brown. He pumps Johnny's hand while Emmy clings to his neck and the hounds fawn at his feet. Slavey comes tripping up and strikes a pretty pose, head tilted, toes pointing delicately. Her big brown eyes never waver from Johnny's face.

"Right glad to see you, Appleseed," Mr. Partridge booms. "You planting out this way?"

"Nay, Jerry, I'm scouting. We've had a bit of Indian trouble down Mansfield way."

Every face but Emmy's clouds right over.

Mr. Partridge asks, "Any action?"

"Some. There's been talk of the British inciting the Indians from Fort Detroit. In August, Captain Pipe and his band were moved out of Jerometown."

"Good thinking." Mr. Partridge approves.

"Then last week Colonel Kratzer removed the Greentown Indians. They didn't want to go. But Reverend Copus assured them their homes would be safe till they came back."

"The Reverend always had a way with the savages." Mr. Partridge spits in the dust.

"But when they looked back, their homes were burning."

"Hah! Kratzer knows the business!"

"Wasn't Kratzer's doing, and certainly not Copus's! Some over-zealous party took it upon themselves. Ever since, we've had what you call action. Levi Jones was killed in the woods. Mansfield took shelter in the blockhouse while I ran to Mt. Vernon for reinforcements."

"Hey, that's a long run."

"Ran thirty miles that night, warning folks. But Copus left the blockhouse and took his family home. He believed the Indians wouldn't harm him."

"So they finished him off?"

Johnny nods. "Also the Zeymore family. By the way, I saw a party of Wyandots northwest of here."

"We keep the guns loaded."

A neat, spare, red-headed woman has come out of the cabin and joined the adoring group around Johnny. They all look at him like he's the angel Gabriel, and so does she. She asks him, "Who's your friend?"

"Hah." He remembers, and turns toward me. "This is Persis. I bought her from the Wyandots with my last snuff. I was hoping you folks might know her. She doesn't know herself, or where she's from."

I wish I could shrivel up and disappear! All eyes but Slavey's turn to me. Slavey never flickers an inch from contemplating Johnny. But Missus and Emmy and Grannie and Mr. all stare at me. I look down at the dust between my raggy moccasins.

"No," Mr. says slowly. "Don't know her. Never saw her. We heard of Wiggins up north, Wheeler, Adams. Never met any of 'em."

"Wheeler's a name she's remarked," says

Johnny. He adds, "Persis is a right good traveler." Still looking at the dust, I commence to blush. "She saved me from a rattler just this morning."

Quick intake of breaths all round. "Quick as he leaped at me, Persis grabbed up a stick and charged him. He made off in confusion." "You've always been lucky," says Mr. Partridge. Grannie cackles, "The Lord takes care of his own!" It's plain to see, no one gives *me* any credit.

But lo, Missus steps up and takes my hand. "Child," says she, "You're wore out. You come in the house now, let these men stand here and talk all day." She commences to lead me away. "Betty," she commands Slavey, "Come thisaway."

I cast a quick look at Betty. She does not care to come. She would stand and take Johnny into her great cow's eyes all day with pleasure! But she dassn't disobey. One, two steps backward she takes, and turns slowly away. Unwilling, she follows Missus and me.

Chapter 6.

INSIDE IS WARM AND DIM. Coals glow in the fireplace. With one hand Missus guides me there. With the other she grabs a stool and sets it right by the coals and pushes me onto it. I don't need much pushing. I fall like a stone.

After woodsy air and falling leaves, the cabin feels a bit like a trap. I think of Wolf, skulking in the woods nearby. Part of me still skulks out there, just waiting for Johnny to break free of these folk and march.

But the trap is comforting. Lo, the safe, shadowed walls! The relaxing warmth! The heavenly smell! There's meat in the kettle on the hearth, and garden stuff, besides corn.

Missus leans over me. "Persis, are you hungry?"

"Aye, M'am!"

She fills a bowl with the wonderful stew. It's meat all right, and potatoes, and cabbage, and squash! I sniff it with joy, but my stomach turns over.

"You're half starved," says Missus. "Don't rush it. You've got all day and night." She's right. With these four walls around, and nobody going to rush at me with teeth or tomahawk, I can take my time. I start with little small spoonfuls.

Dimly, I notice Missus and Betty skipping about. They fetch a dress, much-washed and patched, but better than my outfit. They draw the moccasins off my sore feet and turn them in the light, clucking and shaking their heads. They fetch a "new" pair. They fetch water and clean rags and set them handy. As I finish the stew, Missus fetches a real eastern silver-edged mirror and props it against the wall. Watery-wavery in the glass, I see myself. I lean to it, and stare.

Lo! Compared to Johnny and Missus and Betty, I *am* chunky. Johnny's right about that. I've got pretty hair, gold like autumn leaves, ripply. But loose now, and tangled with twigs and burrs. My arms and neck are briar-scratched. My skirt is ripped so it's barely decent.

I look in my own eyes. My eyes are gray and wide and cold. No feeling shows. *I* don't show. Nobody looking at those eyes knows anything about me, and that's fine. I like that. I like myself tolerable well.

Missus says, "Stand up, Child, take off those rags you're wearing." While Betty stands guard at the door, she helps me undress and wash. Then she drops the "new" dress over my head. "This is Betty's old dress . . . I was going to use it in my new hooked rug, but . . . Reckon that's how I will use it. It's too thin for you by half!"

She fetches Grannie's old skirt. Grannie must have thinned out recent, for this old skirt nearly stretches round me. "Take a strip from your old dress, Betty, and piece it to this." Missus finds me a buckskin shirt, too, that was Danny's. Whoever Danny is.

One lone ax keeps ringing out back.

Betty brings a stool by mine and sets to work piecing. Missus hands me a comb. "Do what you can with your hair, Child." She goes out.

Betty coughs. She asks, "You been traveling long with Appleseed John?"

"A day and a night, about."

"What's he like on the trail?"

"Fast! I been running all that time, 'cept when we slept."

"Where was that?"

"In a tree."

"Does he preach on the trail?"

Hah. "If that's what you call it, aye. Some. He says some strange things."

Betty heaves a sigh, and coughs. "Appleseed John's the finest man you'll ever meet," she declares.

I see she envies me my travel with Johnny. Maybe she thinks she'd rather run after him through briar and brush than sweep and churn for Missus Partridge! I puff up a bit, being envied.

Half the burrs are out of my hair, and it commences to shine in the mirror. Betty hands me the pieced skirt and I stand up and step into it. It surely feels good, standing up in whole moccasins and skirt and a good, soft, old buckskin, and all on a full stomach!

"He's not the handsomest man you'll meet," Betty murmurs.

"No," say I, "He's not." I'm thinking of that twitchy nose and yellow tooth, and the feet hard as hoofs.

"But he's the sweetest. Everyone loves Johnny. And the stories he tells! What I'd give to sit by a campfire and hear Johnny's stories all night!" Betty coughs, and jumps up. "I'm going to see what he's up to now! Want to come?"

I shake my head. "What I'd give to sit withindoors by a stewpot!"

"Help yourself," Betty offers grandly. "There's plenty stew." She trips to the door.

A peek in the pot shows, truly, a plenty stew. I refill my bowl.

Out back, the lone ax rings and rings. Someone has not quit work to admire Johnny. "Betty," I ask, for she still stands tippytoe at the door, "Who's that chopping?"

"Why, that's Black Ross. And look, there's Appleseed John!" Betty coughs and flutters like a brown bird out into the sunlight.

Chapter 7.

FIRELIGHT LEAPS ON THE HEARTH. Candles waver on the table. Dinner cleared, the Partridges gather by the hearth. Grannie and Missus take stools, Grannie still puffing away at her pipe. Mr. sits on the front log with Danny, who looks sixteen. Emmy and Betty sit on the floor. The place by the fire is left empty.

"Hss, Girl." Grannie signals to me. "Sit yourself down." She points her pipe at the floor by Betty. Betty pushes over a bit and I fold myself down beside her. She coughs in the gathering silence. Everyone looks toward the door.

It opens. Two figures come into the firelight. Johnny, heavy Bible in hand, and a black man. Black Ross.

He is stooped, white haired, wiry. He stands uncertainly in shadow. Mr. Partridge starts to speak. "Humph!" He starts. But Johnny interrupts.

" 'Among the Gentiles in Heaven,' " he intones in his grandest voice, " 'The most beloved are the Africans. They accept good and true elements of Heaven more readily than others.' "

I reckon Black Ross is an African. I reckon and feel, from the breathing and stirring around me, that he's not expected to join the Partridge gathering.

Mr. Partridge growls, and sinks into silence. Missus beckons Black Ross. He squeezes in between me and Emmy. Like me, he shrinks down small so as not to be noticed. We glance at each other sideways. Ross's face is rugged. His chestnut-colored eyes are sad. He flicks me a secret, sad smile, and I answer it.

His veiny, old hand, resting by mine, is very dark. I feel weird about that. It reminds me of ... Indians, I reckon. I want to draw my hand away, but I don't move an inch. I wouldn't sadden Ross for another bowlful of stew!

Johnny steps carefully among us all to the empty place by the fire. Little Emmy commences to scramble toward him, but Betty grabs her dress and pulls her back. Johnny lies down comfortably facing us, resting on his elbow, with the Bible open before him. Missus sets a candle beside him, and Johnny commences to read in a fine, high tone.

" 'A man is such as the quality of his love is. If

there be with a man the love of God and the love of the Neighbor he is, as to his spirit, which lives on after death, an angel; no matter how he appears in the external world.' "

An angel. Such as Johnny promised to show me. Of course, he's done no such thing.

I look carefully at Johnny as he reads on and on, and everyone listens like it was Judgement Day. Back in the woods I didn't much notice how he appeared in the external world. But here I compare his bare feet with Mr. Partridge's boots. Even Ross has boots! And I compare his tin mushpot with the cloth caps hanging yonder behind the door. And as for the coffee sack he walks around in! No two ways to take it, Johnny appears strange in the external world.

But as to his spirit, which the books says lives on after death, that is certainly an angel. Love of God and the Neighbor and the Creature is with Johnny. He bought me from the Wyandots with his last snuff. (That's what he keeps forgetting, when he opens his snuffbox.) He helped Wolf out of the pit and took on poor old Peg, whose owner wouldn't feed him because he was useless. Johnny is either an angel or a crazy, or maybe both. It's all most of us can do to take care of ourselves, never mind strangers and animals!

While my thoughts wander, the fire has burned low. Now Johnny reads, " 'There is but one life which is the Lord's, and this life flows in and causes man to live. All those throughout the world who have lived in good are, of the Lord's mercy, received and saved.' " Johnny shuts the book on his thumb and looks around at us. "And that includes all folks, even Indians."

The Partridges gasp.

Grannie asks, "What did he say?"

Missus repeats, "Even Indians, he says."

Grannie shakes her old head till the white hairs rise like milkweed seed. "Not even Appleseed John can tell me Indians go to Heaven!"

Mr. says firmly, "The only good Indian is a dead Indian."

Johnny opens his snuffbox. He looks in it with that sad surprise he should be used to by now, and closes it.

Mr. says, "Johnny, you'll get in trouble trusting Indians! I know you run around with 'em, visit their towns like Christian cabins. It's said you've been seen at their, er, ceremonies. But you can't trust 'em. One day they'll bury a tomahawk in your head, like they did poor old Copus."

"Poor old Copus didn't use his head," Johnny argues. "He should have known the Indians would blame him when their town was burned. They thought he lied to them. He promised their homes would be safe, and they burned down before their owners were out of sight! He should never have left the blockhouse."

He goes on to say, "Nor can you blame the Indians for thinking he lied. Every wicked deed of the Indians, Jerry, is matched by a wicked deed of our own. Why, an innocent old man, a Wyandot, came to fetch his daughter who was visiting in Greentown. He fetched her away. But two soldiers hunted them down and wounded him. The daughter escaped. The old man fell wounded into the creek, and they came up and killed him with his own tomahawk. As harmless a fellow as myself. There's good and evil, Jerry, in the heart of every man, no matter his color.

"And that reminds me. Have you folks decided what you'll do? I'll guide you to the Mansfield blockhouse, if you wish."

Mr. Partridge asks, "What exactly's the situation?"

"The situation appears to be . . . I would mightily appreciate a pinch of snuff!"

Missus produces a pinch, which Johnny enjoys.

"The Indians were on the move because of land-takings, injustices, Tecumseh and the Prophet. But since Greentown was burned and other vengeances exacted, they've been quieter. In my scouting, I met only this one band of Wyandots."

Missus asks, "Is it true that the British are inciting the savages against us?"

"Maybe, M'am. They certainly are selling them guns. But in my opinion, things are quieting down. You'd likely be safer here on your land than traipsing with me through the wilderness."

"Well," says Mr. "We'll decide overnight."

Everyone rises. Johnny takes the heavy Bible he was reading from and tears it right in half, like I would tear one page of it. He hands one half to Mr. "Keep this till I come again," he says. "Read from it. Teach Emmy her letters with it."

Missus asks, "But what will you do with half a book, Johnny?"

"I'll leave it with someone else. Then when next I come, I'll bring you this half and take your half to him."

Emmy runs to Johnny. He picks her up for a goodnight kiss, then makes for the door. Ross shuffles after him, hoping not to be noticed. But Grannie notices. "For a good Christian," she remarks, "Johnny's got weird ways! Will he sleep in the shed with Ross?"

"Maybe," Missus says. "More likely he'll sleep outside. He doesn't care for a roof over him."

She picks up Johnny's candle from the hearth and hands it to me. "Persis, you sleep in the loft with Betty. I've spread extra quilts."

Grannie knocks out her pipe on the hearth. Missus snuffs candles. Mr. bars the door with three bolts.

"It's peculiar," Missus says, heading for the big bed in the corner, "I plan to sleep tonight, Indians or no Indians! With Appleseed Johnny sleeping yonder, I feel no ill can come near the house. It's as if an angel watched over us."

Mr. Partridge says, "Humph!"

47

Chapter 8.

WARM IN SOFT QUILTS, Betty's maddening cough comes back. I hope she won't cough in my ear all night! She won't keep me awake, though, I doubt I've ever been this comfortable in my life! It's like Johnny's Heaven. Safe roof over, thick quilt under! Johnny must be crazy to sleep outside. But then, of course we know, Johnny *is* crazy.

Betty murmurs between coughs, "I've got my eye on Johnny."

"Eh?"

"Had my eye on him for years."

"You mean, you've set your cap for him?"

"Aye, that's what I mean. (Cough.) Such a wunnerful *good* man! And must be lonesome, wandering the woods."

"I don't know about that." There's something

cool, distant, about Johnny. I doubt he minds being lonesome.

"Not that he'd be much of a husband, by everyone's taste. Funny ways to him. Sleeps outdoors. Never eats meat. Dresses like Emmy's cornhusk doll. But I reckon if he married, all that would change. He'd settle down in his own place. Grow apples in his own field. Stick to home like a Christian."

I doubt. "Do you like him that much, Betty?"

"I like him a lot. Can't very well not like Johnny! And then, I'd get away from here." Cough.

"Are the Partridges mean?"

"Lord, no! Good folks. I've no complaint. But a girl just naturally wants her own man, and hearth, and cradle." *Thirteen years I was a daughter.*

"Well, is Johnny interested?" Sure doesn't seem it.

"He's never looked at me different from Emmy, or the cat! Johnny's good to all. It's just there's no other man around here to think on."

Betty sighs, coughs and turns away, pulling the quilt with her. I yank it firmly back. She mumbles, "Can't say Johnny's handsome . . . If we go to Mansfield tomorrow I may meet someone there . . . younger."

"How old is Johnny?"

"Thirty-five if he's a day." (Cough. Snore.)

Betty breathes deep and slow. I commence to sink toward sleep. Just before I get there it hits me, like lightning. I tighten right up, eyes wide open on the dark.

Betty's out of luck.

It's *me* Johnny means to wed.

It explains everything! Why he paid his last snuff—and how Johnny loves his snuff—to buy me from Owner. Why he's bringing me through the wilderness, sharing his rations and all. He said I was good looking, didn't he? Liked my pretty gold hair, didn't he? I blush to remember!

Aye, Johnny Appleseed wants to marry me! We'll raise a cabin and farm a field and sit by our hearth, just the two of us!

Maybe "just the two of us" is asking a bit much. There will certainly be children. Johnny seems to like them. And I reckon our cabin will shortly fill up with out-of-luck folks and animals. We'll have a crowd, if Johnny gets his way.

And he will! I'll be good to Johnny. By jingo, I'll be the best wife ever spun flax! Because I know what it is to be alone, and cut off from the world.

My eyes sink shut. Betty breathes warm beside me. My mind wanders down the ladder and looks at Mr. and Missus Partridge in the big bed, and Emmy in the trundle bed. I don't know where Danny sleeps. My mind drifts out through the door bolted three times, and finds Black Ross curled on his pallet in the shed. Peg munches moonlit grass outside. Away in the woods Wolf prowls and waits.

Appleseed John lies under a dooryard lilac. A

soft light surrounds him, moonlight or halo. Missus is right. With Johnny asleep yonder, no ill can come near the house. An angel watches over us.

Chapter 9.

I'M DANDLING THIS INFANT. A tiny boy, three or four months old. He's laughing like a fool and waving his arms, and I'm counting his toes for him. We sit by a window where a wind drifts in—it's a sizzle-hot day—and we have a bucko time till, lo, a witch darkens the doorway.

My stomach grabs up at sight of her. She's old, forty, five times my chunky size, snorting and sweating like a draft horse. She bowls through that door like a raging she-bear, grabs the broom, shakes it at us. "Get off that bench, you lazy brat!" She yells. "Get out to the mowing before Mister comes looking for his lunch!"

Aye, that's what I came in here for, Mister's lunch. But I found Baby crying, and one thing led to another. No use trying to explain to Witch. I think of Mr. Wheeler waiting in the mowing, scything, watching for his lunch, angry. I don't care to go out there in the heat, to Mr. Wheeler! Just to get away I open my eyes.

My name is Persis. I am fourteen.

I'm lying bare and alone under a soft quilt. Betty's gone. Sunlight pours through a small dust-framed window, and so does Johnny's voice. He must be talking right underneath.

"That's a wise decision," he says. "I don't expect much more trouble myself, and you've got a lot to lose here. Better stay and take care of it." I reckon the Partridges are not coming with us. Betty will be disappointed, but I'm glad.

"Now about this here Pegasus," Johnny goes on. "He's a good old codger. Won't give you any trouble. If you could just keep him till spring. You know that I will repay his costs on my return."

Mr. Partridge says, "I don't know where you get your money, Johnny, but you always come up with it."

"I get it from honest business, Jerry, same as you."

"What do you do, hide money in hollow trees in your orchards?"

"Will you keep old Peg for me?"

"I'd like to favor you, but not that way. Remember that ancient roan you saddled me with last time?"

"Old Priam. I've been meaning to inquire after

him and pay his costs."

"He didn't last the week. No costs to pay. But I don't fancy carving up another skeleton for dog-food."

"Peg here is in pretty good shape. A little rest and a handful of corn..."

"On the other hand, and changing the subject. If you'd like to leave the girl, Priscilla."

"That's Persis."

I sit up. The quilt slides off me. Johnny wouldn't leave me here! Then I remember, he wants to marry me. I take an easier breath, and I hear him say...

"Persis, now, she's in powerful shape! A sturdy young creature with her heart in the right place. You'd take care of her?"

I'm on my feet.

"Need you ask, John! You know I care for all that's mine."

" 'The just man cares for his beast.' "

Hey, Johnny, is that a way to talk about your intended? I'm fighting my way into my new pieced skirt.

"You are a just man, Jerry," Johnny says. "It rejoices my heart to see you prosper in the ways of virtue! But you need to know this about Persis. There's no paper on her. She doesn't know who she is. There may be legal problems."

Legal problems be hanged! You're not leaving your bride-to-be, Johnny Appleseed! I dive into the buckskin shirt.

"I'll chance that," Mr. Partridge says. "Betty's down more often with the cough now, and Missus has extra work just taking care of her. An extra pair of hands . . ."

In one hand I grab my moccasins. I fly down the ladder. I swear, my feet never touch the rungs. Betty looks up from the hearth. I'm out the door.

In the sunny dooryard, Peg stands swishing his tail. His nose droops on Johnny's shoulder. Johnny's got his walking stick in hand. You'd think he might blush, seeing me hurtle out the door, but he never blinks. A yellow cat winds around his feet.

He wrinkles his nose. "Ask her yourself," he tells Mr. Partridge. "Here she is."

Mr. Partridge clears his throat. "Would you like to stop here and work along of Betty?" he asks me. "You'd be pretty safe here. I'll give you bed and board, and after the Trouble's over, I'll try to find your folks."

I get it! I get it! Johnny's doing a good action. He wants to take me along to Mansfield and marry me, but he also wants to help the Partridges out. They need a slavey, and Johnny's got me. Typical Johnny. Well, I'm not going to be his good action!"

I say firmly, "Johnny, I'm going with you."

Johnny twinkles at me. I think he looks relieved. But all he says is, "Then let us be off."

But at this instant up come Missus and Emmy, with Betty at their heels. Betty strikes a pose for

Johnny's benefit. She draws an old red shawl over her shoulders and lets it drape gracefully. Betty hasn't guessed the real situation yet.

Missus hand me a basket, with little parcels wrapped in cornhusks. "I know Johnny can march all day without food and think nothing of it," she says. "But you will need dinner."

"Thank you, M'am!" With all my heart!

"You may feel better with this." She lays a long-handled knife in the basket. "We can't all count on angelic protection."

"Thank you, M'am!"

Turning to Betty, Missus holds out a hand. Crestfallen, Betty slips off the red shawl and hands it over. That goes in the basket too. "That's for a blanket tonight."

"Missus," say I, "I can't thank you enough." And that's fact.

Johnny stoops to kiss Emmy. She tries to cling, but he straightens up fast. "Goodby, Emmy," he says. "Learn your letters before I come back. God bless the house!" And we're off.

Peg wears a "new" halter. Probaby old Priam's halter. I lead him by a greasy leather rein. Thud, thud, go the patient hoofs on the hard-trodden trail. Woods close in around us. Bright leaves swish by, red and yellow and brown. The trail leads up, then down. Sun, shade, speckled sun. Sun, shade, speckled sun. And always Johnny's narrow back, just vanishing around the next bend.

Chapter 10.

LO, WOLF COMES FRISKING about Johnny, grinning and slinking and rolling over. Johnny greets him friendly, but never slacks his pace. I wish he would sit down and converse with Wolf so I could sit too! I ache all over again, and my "new" moccasins are wearing down.

Peg wishes it too. I know because he blows as the trail rises, and stumbles when it dips. And his head bobs lower each time I glance back.

Fact, Wolf is a handsome beast. His coat shines reddy-brown in the speckled sunlight. His eyes are bright and, right now, gentle. Though I remember well they can glow and glare. I'm glad he's back with us. I feel safer with him, more complete. As though I had my family about me.

Johnny rounds a bend in the trail. I and Peg

come to the bend, and lo! No Johnny.

Wolf bounds onto the trail from the right, sees us and bounds back. I lead Peg to the right.

We come against a high brush fence built of branches, logs and wedged limbs. A narrow stick gate has been lifted back. It's just wide enough so I can lead Peg through.

Here stand great girdled dead trees, as far as I can see. Among them spring saplings, as high as my waist. Fruit trees.

Apples! Of course! This is Johnny's work. And here he sits on a log, waiting for dinner. Wolf lies farther off, half hidden in brown leaves.

Gratefully, I sit down beside Johnny. Peg blows tiredly and lets his head sink to the ground.

I divide Missus Partridge's little packets between me and Johnny. Journeycake, onions, roast potatoes! We munch in silence. Peg finds the strength to wander away through the orchard, trailing his lead.

First hunger satisfied, I doubt that Johnny may leap up ready to go. To keep him sitting, I ask him how he makes an orchard like this.

The telling takes a time, as I hoped it would. First, he went to a cider mill in a faraway place called Pennsylvania, and collected apple seeds from the sludge. Then he walked here, a many-days hike. This land he simply uses. No one owns it. Other orchards he leases, and some he actually owns.

Next thing, he girdled all these trees. "I can girdle twice as many trees twice as fast in a day as any man I know," he boasts. I believe it. Then he planted his apple seeds among the dying trees. Through the bare branches the sun reached the seedlings, and they throve. "These are five years old. Almost time to sell." The last touch was the brush fence, to keep out hogs and deer.

Every so often Johnny comes by to weed and prune his trees. He never, never grafts them. "You can improve the apple that way, but that is only a device of man. It's wicked to cut up good trees that way! The correct method is to select good seeds and grow them in good ground, and let God alone improve the apples."

I ask, What does he do with the money he makes? For I don't see that he has much of this world's goods.

"Money?" says he. "Money. Hah! That reminds me."

He gets up. My heart sinks into my aching feet! But Johnny walks only a little way, to one of the great dead trees. He reaches inside it through a woodpecker hole, and lifts out a tattered, grimy pouch.

"Lucky I had this money here," he says cheerfully. "I reckon we'll have to pay someone to keep old Peg for the winter. I'm going to look around here, Percy. You rest till I'm back. Take a nap." He turns and strides away. In a moment he has disappeared among dead trunks and yellow-leafed seedlings.

A wind rises. A few orange leaves fly past. I am alone in these woods. No Johnny. No Wolf, even; he's vanished. I almost leap up and run in search of Johnny.

Most like I wouldn't find him. And he's left his leather bag here on the log by me. He'll come back for that, if not for me.

Curious, I open the bag. I lift out two Bibles, torn in half. Also flints, tinder, a small hatchet, a big needle, coarse thread, a sack of . . . seeds. This is what Johnny travels with.

I put his wealth back in the bag and fish another potato out of the basket.

Munching, I watch Peg graze in the open orchard. He's found a patch of clover in the sunny space. He moves along slow, switching his tail, shaking his mane. Sunset turns his wide white side pink.

Peg looks up, points his ears. Blows. Peg sees something I don't see.

I hear, though. Twigs snap off to the left.

I put my potato down on the log and fetch the long-handled knife out of Missus Partridge's basket. Gripping this I stand up for a look-see.

Something small and brown moves behind a sapling. Yonder, something rustles and rushes about, urging it forward. Wolf.

A very small brown boy steps into the sunset

light and stands blinking.

What is a youngster doing out here alone, dressed in a little homespun shirt and moccasins and nothing else?

He stares at me with dark round eyes. His soft lips tremble. Black hair falls straight to his shoulders. He's two or three years old, no more.

"Hey, Boy," I say. "Where'd you come from?"

He doesn't answer. Wolf sneaks closer behind him. He edges forward a bit, no closer to me. Wolf snaps his teeth.

Wolf expects me to eat him! I can't help laughing. "What's your name, Boy?"

He doesn't answer.

I get it! Lightning flashes in my mind. Lo! "You're Indian!"

In a trice, I'm up top of the log as if I'd seen a snake. The knife flashes in my fist. The Indian boy stares, swaying on little plump legs.

Indian is a word like *wolf,* meaning dangerous. But, fact, there's nothing dangerous about this youngster. I'm the dangerous one, teetering on this log, knife gleaming.

I remember my dream of Missus Wheeler, where she waved her broom at me and glared. Missus Wheeler was a hard, mean woman, and now I am like her. The youngster sees me like her, mean and hard and fierce.

I drop the knife in the basket and step down off the log. I make for the youngster. He tries to back off but Wolf snaps at his heels. I gather him up, sit him on the log and kneel before him, trapping him. I dig the last journeycake out of the basket. We get on fine. He's munching away like he's starving when a shadow falls across us. My Indian looks up at Johnny. He takes Johnny in with his wide dark stare. Then he goes on eating. Johnny sits down and wiggles his nose. "The woods are getting crowded," he remarks. "Me, I've always been a loner. Now I seem to be collecting a family. We'll call this one Brownie for now. Alright, Brownie?"

The child looks past the cake in his fists and smiles.

Johnny talks to him a bit in Indian, but seems to get nowhere. Brownie's Indian is baby-talk.

I say, "It will be dark soon. (Darkness can be romantic. And Johnny's mind is running on Family! Maybe tonight he will pop the question.) "Can I make a fire for us here?" (Firelight can be romantic, too.)

"I never make a fire when it's warm. Too many innocent mosquitoes fly in and burn up."

I don't blink. I don't give him the satisfaction. "Well, can I make a fire special for Brownie, so he won't be frightened?"

"Hah. Very well. If you wish."

He gives me the flints from his bag.

"Wolf wanted me to eat Brownie," I tell him.

"Hah! Wolf never heard the Good News Straight

From Heaven. Not his fault."

Wolf creeps quite near Johnny. His doggy gaze is gentle on Johnny's face.

Chapter 11.

MY FIRE GLOWS in its earthen circle. Far off—praise be!—wolves howl. Johnny chuckles. "I love to hear them howl," he remarks. "Makes me feel alive." Wolf sits beyond the firelight, perking his ears.

Johnny amuses Brownie for a while by sticking thorns in his—Johnny's—bare feet. His feet don't appear to notice, never mind hurt. Brownie watches, wide-eyed. Later, he laughs. Still later, he falls asleep, head on Johnny's knee.

This is the time for Johnny to pop his question about marriage. But he's been silent. I must lead him to it. I'm beginning to wonder if Johnny is shy!

I start off by asking, "What will you do with Brownie?"

He shrugs. "I know a Delaware town not far off.

Hidden. I hope I'm the only white man knows it. We'll take him there. Maybe that's his home. Or maybe they'll adopt him."

"What! We're going there?"

"Tomorrow. It's not far out of our way."

Now, this is alarming! I've just escaped the clutches of one batch of Painted Men. I don't want to meet another! "Won't they scalp us?"

"They're old friends of mine."

I have to believe him. Wolf is a friend of his, why not Delawares? "Those Wyandots you bought me from. Were those old friends of yours too?"

"Never saw them before in my life. But that was a safe bet. They thought I was crazy." (You don't say!) "Indians won't harm a crazy. They think God protects him, and they're probably right."

All this is interesting, but not getting us to the point, which is marriage. I say, "Johnny, you never saw me before either. Why did you take a chance and go out among them and buy me?" Now he can mention my pretty golden hair and go on from there.

He says, " 'Good actions ought to be done because they are of God and from God and lead us to Heaven.' "

By jingo, he's on his high horse again! "Johnny, where do you get all this Bible talk? It sounds like Bible, and then it doesn't."

Surprised, Johnny wiggles his nose. "Bible talk? It's not Bible. It's Swedenborg."

"What?"

"Emanuel Swedenborg."

"Who?"

Johnny says Emanuel Swedenborg lived long ago in a faraway place called Sweden. He saw visions and wrote them down in books. These are the books Johnny carries around in his bag. I didn't know there were any books but the Bible. Johnny says, "Many. 'Of the making of many books there is no end.' But these of Swedenborg's are the best."

"What did this Swedenborg do besides write books?"

"Eh?"

"Was he a farmer or a peddler or an orchardman?"

"Far as I know, writing was what he did." Sounds like a right strange man and a right strange life.

"How do you know these visions of his are true?

"Why, I feel them. Here." Johnny touches his heart.

This is interesting, but not getting us any nearer to marriage.

"Johnny," I say point-blank, "You're going to take Brownie to the Delawares. You're going to pay someone to keep Peg. What about *me*? What are you going to do with *me*?"

"Hah." He stares into the fire. My heart sets up a quick tremble. Here it comes!"

"If you can remember your folks, I'll take you to them, no matter where."

"You know I don't remember nothing." Except that Mama is dead.

"Then I'll have to take you to the Mansfeld blockhouse. Someone there may know you. Or someone may offer you a job. You'll do fine."

What's the matter here? Is Johnny really too shy to say *marry*?

"What makes you think I'll do fine?" Just keep him talking about my good points.

"You're a good strong girl, Percy, though a bit skinnier than when we met. And good-looking."

This is better. I blush happily.

"You have much to offer life, and life will offer you much. You will perform uses."

I would like to perform these uses right here, or a bit closer to Civilization, in a cabin we could build together. We could all stay here, Johnny and me and Peg and Wolf and even Brownie, if the Delawares don't want him. We could be a family. I try to hold Johnny's eyes with mine and make him see it, but he's staring into the fire.

"You know why I like you, Percy?" he says suddenly. Ah, this sounds promising! "I like you for your name. My sister's name is Persis. She's not much older'n you."

Sister! "Johnny, you have a family?" The thought has never entered my head! I didn't think a family would *let* a man wander the woods in a coffeesack, with a mushpot hat!

By jingo, aye, Johnny has a family! His father

died lately, but his stepmother still lives near Marietta with many of his ten half-brothers-and-sisters.

"Stepmother? Aye, I remember you said you lost your mother," I say, all sympathy. "Like I did."

He doesn't remember her. He was two when she died, while his father was off fighting for Washington. That was in a faraway land called Massachusetts. He says, "It's all right, Persis. She's an angel now."

"How do you know she's an angel?"

"She was good," he says simply. "My Pa kept a letter she wrote him before she died." He recites it. " 'Remember I beseech you that you are mortal and consider that we are always in danger of our spiritual enemy. Be therefore on your guard continually and live in a daily preparation for death. I hope we shall both be as happy as to spend an eternity of happiness together in the coming world, which is my desire and prayer." Well, now," says he, "Don't you suppose the woman who penned those words is now in Heaven?"

Fact, words and deeds don't always match like tongue and groove. But this is Johnny's *mother* we're talking about, so I make no remark on that.

"Fact," I say, "She's an angel. Like the one you promised to show me."

"Hah. I remember. I did promise."

"That's all right. You don't have to."

"Oh, but I will! I said I would show you an angel,

and I will do so. Tomorrow."

"Whatever you say, Johnny."

He settles his knapsack under his head. Quick, quick, I grab one last chance to get him to pop that question.

"Johnny, you like young'uns."

"Aye."

"Why don't you marry and have your own?"

He rolls his eyes at me, dark and serious. "Percy," he says, "Not all women are virtuous. A man could make a terrible mistake., And hell itself is no worse than a smoky house and a scolding wife."

"But, Johnny," I take the bull by the horns. "I know how to make a fire that won't smoke. And I wouldn't be a scolding wife, not me!" There. How much plainer can I hint?

Johnny smiles at me and closes his eyes. "You will make some man a fine wife, Percy. I see you now as you will one day be, grown old and gray in loving service and Heavenly uses. Then all who look in your faded face will see Heaven waiting there, behind the wrinkles."

Which must be the least romantic speech any girl ever heard from the lips of man!

Chapter 12.

IN A SMALL, SHADOWED ROOM an old man writes at a table. He wears a dark, worn dressing gown, and sips coffee as he writes. He is small and thin, with wild, white hair. His eyes are deep and thoughtful. He is Johnny's Swedenborg.

Swedenborg stops writing. He sets his quill in its holder and gathers his papers in a neat pile. Quick and agile, he stands up and sheds his dressing gown. Under it he wears a dark suit. He slaps a wig of white curls on top of his own white hair, and strides out the door.

Lo, a garden, bright with flowers and bushes I never saw before. Swedenborg works at a table, planting seeds in a box of earth.

I draw near. He looks up and smiles, his thin face lighting up cheerfully, though his eyes remain serious. Cupping seeds in his two hands he says, "So full of Divine Love and Divine Wisdom is the universe, it may be said to be Divine Love and Divine Wisdom in image."

Lo, a weird dream!

Chapter 13.

BRIGHT LEAVES SWISH PAST, red and yellow and brown. The trail leads up, then down. Sun, shade, speckled sun. Sun, shade, speckled sun. And always Johnny's narrow back, just vanishing around the next bend.

Thud, thud, go Peg's patient hoofs behind me. Brownie rides him, clinging to his mane. "Such a little weight won't bother," Johnny said, lifting Brownie on. At first his lips trembled and his wide dark eyes opened even wider. But now when I glance back he is smiling. He grasps a hunk of mane in each fist and drums his small heels on Peg's threadbare ribs. Peg doesn't seem to mind.

Off to our right, thrashing thickets show where Wolf trots.

We catch up with Johnny. He's standing on the

bank of a little pool, gone thoughtful. He turns to us smiling, and crinkles his nose. "Now, Percy, I'll show you an angel."

What exactly does he mean by that? If there's an angel in that pool under the floating leaves, I'm not at all sure I want to see him! I hang back.

Johnny lifts Brownie down off Peg. Peg notices water and stumbles in to drink. Ripples flow across the pool. "Come on, Percy. You wanted to see an angel."

A tall black willow leans over the pool. Johnny takes my hand and sets it on a low branch. "Hang on. Lean over. Now, look. It's in the water."

All right. I'm hanging on, leaning and looking. In the pool the ripples smooth out so I can see my face. Leaves float across it. It looks up at me, puzzled, like I feel.

My face is thinner than in the Partridge mirror. My eyes are wide as Brownie's, my braid's a real mess, yellow and rough as the floating leaaves. And where is Johnny's angel?

"There!" he says, triumphant. "You see!"

"No, I don't."

"You will."

I go on looking, hunting for the angel.

Peg blows a mighty "SCHOOF!" and gallops up on the bank.

Johnny says, "By jingo!"

I feel a scrit-scratching traveling through the bark under my hand. I step back and look up.

A half-grown bear cub is climbing down the willow. It pauses to stare at us. Brownie laughs. "Makatut!" He calls happily. Or some such word.

The little bear looks round at us with eyes as round as Brownie's. Fact, there is a resemblance. I have to laugh, too.

"Come on down, Fella," Johnny calls to it. And lo, it comes! It hitches backwards down the trunk and stands among us.

Johnny capers about. The cub capers after him. He commences to somersault and stand on his head for the cub's admiration. Brownie's laughter peals over the pond.

CRASH! goes something away in the alders.

Peg snorts, half rears, and takes to his heels.

Brownie's laughing cuts off like with a knife. He dives for the willow and scrambles straight up the trunk to where the cub was. In a trice, he's perched on a branch screeching, "Eekee! Eekee!" Or some such word.

Alders to our right shake like in a high wind. Something groans and growls, coming fast. Brownie wails.

Me, I'm whirling round and round wondering what to do. I could rush into the pond and submerge, like Johnny in the cattails. I could grab a stick—there is no stick—and stand beside Johnny. Possibly in front of him. I could melt quietly into the alders to my left.

What decides me is the smell that now wafts

over us. It's sickening. It screams, Danger!

"*Eekee!*" Brownie sounds hoarse.

I don't think about it. One minute I'm whirling like a square dance on the bank. Next minute, lo, I'm perched on Brownie's willow branch. No notion how I got there.

Johnny stands below us, calm as the pool itself. I'm looking down on his shiny mushpot hat. Beside him, the cub stands up on hind feet.

"Johnny!" I yell. *"Do something!"*

The she-bear breaks cover.

She rears to stand like a person, weaving her wet black snout in the air. Her little eyes squint in the watery light. She grunts, and rakes the air with fearsome claws. She's thick around as a maple trunk, dark-furred, cumbersome. She doesn't seem to see Johnny, but her nose turns toward him.

The cub drops on all fours and scuttles over to Mama.

She sniffs him over. Then she wallops him one. He rolls away. Mama drops, and heads for Johnny.

"Johnny! *Johnny!*" Someone screams. I think it's me.

Johnny just stands.

Halfway to him, the she-bear pauses. She sits down and scratches at her shoulder. She whines. The cub scampers up to her, whimpering.

Wolf stands at the edge of the alders. Stiff-furred, ears perked, he fixes the bear with eyes as evil as her own.

75

Johnny says quietly, "Your baby's fine. We were just funning."

Wolf sneaks three slow steps forward.

The bear heaves up. She makes for Johnny again. Wolf crouches, wiggling, ready to launch.

Lo, the bear walks around Johnny and into the alders. The cub follows. The last we see of them is his little round backside, bobbing away.

Wolf stands up.

The smell lifts and drifts away.

Brownie and I are silent. My throat feels torn from screaming.

Johnny cocks back his mushpot and wrinkles his nose at us. "You look like a pair of owlets! Bet you don't know how you got up there."

Right. And more important, I don't know how we'll get down.

"Peg and I'll get you down," says Johnny. "I'll have to stand on his poor old back for a minute. Then we'll mend your skirt, Percy."

I glance down at my skirt. Pieced new at Partridge's day before yesterday, it's rags now.

Chapter 14.

WE TRAVEL THROUGH THICKETS without a trail. Brownie has to lie flat on Peg's back or be swept off by swishing branches. I have to lead Peg around trees and bushes and watch out for windfalls. Even Johnny travels slow. Wolf slinks close by.

"Guess this place we're going sure is secret!" I remark to a passing oak.

"Sure is!" Johnny answers, ahead. "You want to remember that, Percy, and never tell a living soul where you've been."

"Never doubt." I don't *know* where I've been.

Light ahead. Girdled trees and burned spaces open before us. We're marching among spaded hills, each with its dry brown cornstalk. Bean vines climb the stalks. Squash vines spread between the hills. Most of everything has been harvested. But lo, here hides a small ear of red corn. I break it off and hand it up to Brownie. Farther on I find myself a blue ear. I husk and gnaw it on the march.

Wolf drops behind Johnny, behind me, even behind Peg. Glancing back I see him stopped, head high. Sniffing.

We pass a pole rack dripping with braided corn ears hung up to dry. A faint smell of smoke greets us. A faint drum-beat.

Four days ago I was with Indians. Johnny rescued me. Now he's leading me back among them. I doubt to go forward. I doubt even more to lose sight of Johnny. I keep my eyes on his tin hat gleaming in the sun, and march.

A glance back proves what I know. Wolf has vanished. By jingo, how I wish I could vanish!

My heart beats with the drum, louder and harder. Ahead, voices chant. Soft voices, a weird chant. My knees tremble.

"Johnny, are you sure these folk are your friends?"

"Aye, Percy." He strides forward. I think of Reverend Copus, killed by his Indian friends. But I have no choice but to stride forward too.

In a great circle of sun and beaten earth people are dancing. I mean, Indians are dancing. Men. Women and children and old men sit around watching. There must be a hundred Indians here.

"Johnny . . ." He doesn't hear. He's advancing to

the circle.

Peg snorts and jerks back on his lead. Brownie squeaks something happy.

The Indians watching the dance are dressed more or less ordinary, with buckskins and skirts and bonnets. The dancers wear Indian breech clouts and leggings. And the two young men leading the dance are outfitted with masks, jackets and leggings of some pale brown, rough fabric.

Johnny steps into the circle. Gratefully, Peg stops. Little Brownie slides down off him without help and trots after Johnny.

No one seems to notice us but three or four men Johnny talks with, softly, hunkered beside them.

Johnny comes back to me. He whispers, "This is the harvest dance in honor of the Corn Mother. We'll have to wait for a break in the ceremony before we talk. Come sit down, Percy."

Lo, Johnny has made himself known. The watchers have seen me. Many thoughtful black eyes are turned our way right now. And no one has moved to harm us. We're not going to be scalped, at least while the dance lasts.

"Turn Peg loose," Johnny commands. I do so. I follow Johnny into maple shade and we sit together against a sturdy trunk. Peg wanders off to graze the harvested gardens.

I rest my feet. And out in the sun the dance tracks back and forth to the drum's soft boom. Now I see what the leaders' outfits are made of. *Corn-*

husks, of all things!

One by one, two by two, men come to hunker down and murmur with Johnny. They smile, smoke, laugh, share snuff.

Brownie wanders around the circle staring at people. A young woman calls him to her, gives him something to eat out of a basket. He sits down with her, and shortly her arm is around him. There, I think, he's adopted. We can go! I turn to Johnny to point this out, but he is deep in conversation with two old men, heavy smokers. What with the smoke and the heat and the thud, thud of the drum, I doze. I jerk awake, amazed at myself. Fact, I was dozing at an Indian harvest dance!

But these folk do not seem dangerous. I gaze around at quiet faces, some watching the dance, some dozing like I was, and I feel myself the only person left outside this circle. Even Johnny is part of the circle. He talks the lingo, he smokes the pipe. Only I sit outside, alone in my skin, like at the Partridge hearth.

I don't belong here. I didn't belong at Partridges'. Where we're going I won't belong. I'm not part of the world.

Late in the day the drum stops. "They're changing dancers," Johnny tells me. "And now we eat!"

Lo, a great kettle has been heating, and now the crowd moves in on it. The Indians all have their bark bowls. Johnny takes off his mushpot hat and presents it as a bowl, and a woman ladles in steaming white hominy, which we eat standing, with sticks and fingers. I did not know I was so hungry!

An old man, one who smoked with Johnny, makes a speech. He points several times to Johnny and to Brownie, so I reckon he's trying to sell Brownie for us. At the end the woman sitting with Brownie speaks up.

"She wants him," Johnny murmurs. "He is her cousin's son, lost when their village burned."

"Can we go now?"

"I think so. We've stayed long enough for politeness."

But first we go over to Brownie and the woman. He rests cuddled in her lap, their two heads close together. They look up at us and smile with lips and eyes. She wears a rush bonnet and homespun dress. A thick black braid lies like a rope down her shoulder.

Inside my head a mist draws back. Very clear, I see a scene from my past, my long-ago.

Another woman holds another boy on her lap. She leans against an oak trunk, moccasined feet flopped out in front. A hoe leans against the oak too. Hot summer light plays with leaf-shadow across the two faces. Her's is weary, strong, still young under the rush bonnet. His is round and soft. He's younger than Brownie. Her heavy braid is a golden rope in his hands.

Mother and son smile up at me. I bring them welcome water. I see the skin bottle in my own small hands. The woman's smile shows two missing teeth. I say aloud, "Mama!"

She fades away. I am staring down at the Indian woman and Brownie, strangers whom I will never see again. But I have had a Mama, and a brother. I have not always been a stranger in the world. Once I was part of the world.

Chapter 15.

SAYS JOHNNY, "My half-brother Nathaniel was fifteen when I lured him into the woods with me. I was old enough to know better. We camped at my orchard on French Creek. Winter came on and we ran out of rations. I walked to the nearest Civilization for rations, a month's walk it was, there and back. I told Brother he'd do better by himself, just one to feed, till I came back. And so he would have, had he known how! But Brother was raised to farm. Knew little of the woods."

I shiver, thinking of Brother Nathaniel alone in the winter woods, not much older'n me! "What happened to him?"

"He'd have starved, but the Senecas found him."

Worse yet!

"They took him in, fed him, taught him to hunt.

That's when I learned to look friendly on Indians."

I poke up our little fire. It burns near a lean-to, a makeshift contraption of logs and brush. This orchard is close to Civilization. Johnny's sold off most of the trees here, and there's grass for Peg. Wolf stands guard yonder. He came bounding up as I laid the fire and dropped a killed rabbit at Johnny's feet. Now it's roasting, smelling like Heaven. Johnny's nose wiggles and his eyes spark.

I remark, "Betty said you never eat meat."

"Aye," he agrees, licking his chops. "That's true."

"But look at you now! Wolf doesn't look any more eager for this rabbit than you do."

"I never eat *tame* meat, or meat that's been murdered just to eat. I wouldn't want to be eaten, so I don't eat other creatures. If I kill something to defend myself, I eat it. I've eaten bear like that, also serpent. And this rabbit is a gift from Wolf. If I scorned it, he wouldn't understand."

At mention of his name, Wolf looks around like a dog. His ears twitch. A horned owl hoots, close to. I start. Johnny chuckles. "I *love* to hear hooters! They make me feel alive."

I poke up the fire. Time to get back to the important subject. Fact, if I don't get Johnny to propose this night, I doubt that he ever will. We should reach Civilization tomorrow.

"Johnny, you said you have a family. Stepmother, Persis, Nathaniel. Do you live with them?"

"No, I just visit there. I live with a friend named

Palmer, near Mansfield. But once I had my own place." His voice turns dreamy. "A cabin with a garden, and beehives, and an orchard. Travelers coming through would stay the night. In the morning, I'd send them west with seedlings and honey." Just what I thought Johnny's home would be like!

"Why did you leave there?"

"Well, everybody had their apple trees. See, I keep ahead of settlement. New settlers find me right where they come, with apple trees ready to sell."

"Hah! I bet you never sold a tree in your life! You give them away."

"Not so, not so!" Johnny shakes his head till the mushpot falls off. "I take money from such as have it. Of course, if a settler has no money, I may take clothes or cornmeal instead."

"Or nothing?"

"If he has nothing, that's what I take."

I ask slyly, "Are you rich then, Johnny?"

"Not rich. But folks would be surprised to know the land and money I've got." Johnny would not be a bad husband. A girl could do a lot worse.

He takes two sticks and lifts the rabbit out of the fire. He divides it three ways.

"There's two of us," I remind him.

"Mustn't forget Wolf."

The three of us eat eagerly. In a trice, the rabbit's inside us and we're all looking about for more, but there is no more.

Says Johnny, "Persis." He looks serious. "You'd never breathe a word about those Delawares, would you?"

"I told you, I couldn't find them again."

"I'm glad of that. They've got a fine town nearby—or they did have. It may have been burned by now. Sad to see so much hate and terror loose in the land! Settlers and Indians should be friends in this world, as they must be in the next. 'The person who possesses what is good from the Lord is an angel-man.' Also, 'Man becomes a true likeness of Heaven to the extent that he is involved in the good of love and faith.' "

"Fact, I don't see what all this has to do with anything."

"The Indians love God and go to Heaven, same as we do. A wise Delaware once told me that Man has a Spirit, and the body is like a cloak for that Spirit. He said we must take care of our Spirits, and live so that God would take us into his home at the end. He meant Heaven. Fact, his teaching was the same as Swedenborg's."

I don't know about this. But it's sad to see these folk, Indians and settlers, turned against each other. Why don't they sit down and talk over their problems? If it's land they're fighting for, isn't there plenty for all?

Fact, everyone on both sides is much too frightened to talk, and with good reason. Frightened folk are angry folk.

I hear myself say dreamily, "My name is Persis. I am fourteen."

Johnny nods. "That we know."

"I worked for the Wheelers for years. They lived in the burned cabin we found."

"Thought so."

"That grave. 'Thirteen years I was a daughter.' That was the first Missus Wheeler. I worked for the second Missus Wheeler."

"And before that?"

"I lived with Mama and Brother... Kevin... and a man. Mama's dead."

"What was the man's name?"

I stare into the coals. The man's name doesn't come, only a feeling of something bad.

Johnny gets up and stretches. He hoots to the horned owl, but it has flown away. "Never mind, Percy. It will come back in time. See how much you've remembered already! You sleep in the lean-to if you like. I prefer outside."

Rolled in Missus Partridge's shawl under the lean-to, I think a bit more about Mama. I see her strong, plain face again, her gap-toothed smile, her braid like a gold rope. She leans against the oak like part of the oak, the boy in her lap. She rests on the earth like part of the earth. Me, I'm apart, holding the water-skin. Not connected. Like now, cut off.

But time was when I sat in her lap myself, part of the earth and the oak.

Chapter 16.

SUN, SHADE, SPECKLED SUN. Sun, shade, speckled sun. Thud, thud, go Peg's patient hoofs behind me. Ahead, Johnny's narrow back vanishes around the next bend. And everywhere gold and tan leaves fall. We walk through a steady rustling rain of leaves. This night the trees will be bare above a golden floor.

We follow a well-trod trail. Smaller trails lead off east and west, but we keep to the main trail, south. Now and then a smell of smoke drifts to us, or the ring of an ax.

Lo, we come to a real bridge over a stream, built of wooden planks! In the middle of the bridge Johnny stops and turns to Wolf. "Thanks for the escort, Wolf. Thanks for the rabbit. Now that side of the bridge over there is Civilization. Time for us to part company."

Wolf cocks his head and twitches his ears.

"Goodby, Wolf," says Johnny.

Wolf sits down in the leaves. He draws his head down into his shoulders, points his nose to the sky and howls. Peg starts and skitters. His hoofs clatter on the bridge. I start and skitter a bit, myself. Johnny turns and leads off the bridge into Civilization. I pull on Peg's rein and follow him. Wolf howls again, but none of us look back.

The trail leads up, then down. Sun, shade, speckled sun. Thud, thud, go Peg's hoofs, slower and slower. Peg is wearing out. Me, I'm stronger than before. I could go on and on. But Johnny said we were almost to Mansfield now.

"Johnny, where exactly are we going?"

"Do you remember this trail, Percy?"

"Don't remember nothing."

"Then I have to take you to the Mansfield blockhouse."

"Where are *you* going?"

"Why, I'm going home to Palmer's. And I sure hope he's got a full stewpot!"

"Can't I come there too?"

"No, Percy, you can't. Palmer wouldn't understand. But we'll meet again soon."

Ahead, something snorts behind a curtain of falling leaves. Peg stops and blows. Johnny calls softly, "Hey! Who goes there?"

Among twirling yellow leaves, a white kerchief

89

flashes.

"Hello, Doe," says Johnny. He stops. Great dark eyes look at us through the leaves. The doe snorts again, and leaps. Slowly she arcs over a fallen tree into a thicket. Her white tail drifts high, like milkweed silk. Where she stood a buck now stands, head high, regarding us. His antlers are like polished bare branches.

"Just Johnny Appleseed here," Johnny tells him. "But your Missus is right. We humans are seldom up to any good." He starts forward slowly. The buck springs, soars over the windfall, and vanishes. Johnny keeps walking.

Over Johnny's shoulder I see a man. He stands where the deer stood. He's not real, I can see leaves falling right through him. He's round, heavy, in buckskin with a fur cap. His beard's like a grey scarf down his front. He aims a shotgun after the deer. As he pulls the silent trigger a name booms in my head.

"Solomon McKinley!"

Uncle Sol vanishes in the smoke of his gun. Johnny turns back.

"I know a Solomon McKinley."

"He's my uncle. We lived with him." And he was near as bad as the Wheelers. You worked your fingers off for Uncle Sol or you didn't eat.

"Hah!" says Johnny. "Should have remembered! I saw you at McKinley's last time I was there; you were just a tot. We had words, McKinley and I, and I never went back. Well, it's just the next trail right. We'll stop there."

"Do I have to live with him?" I won't!

"Don't fret, Percy. Maybe he knows other relations of yours. We'll see what develops."

Johnny sets off at a trot. I have to call him back. "Peg can't go so fast, Johnny."

"Hah, Pegasus." He comes back and strokes Peg's bony face. Peg whimpers a whinny. "I bet McKinley will keep old Peg, for money."

"Peg might not like that."

"I doubt he can make McKinley's, never mind go farther. And think, Percy. When I come to check up on Peg, I can check up on you, too."

Chapter 17

WE'RE CROSSING our second wood-plank bridge. Clonk, clonk, go Peg's slow hoofs on the planks. A slight brown brook dashes under the bridge. Dreamily, I say, "I thought it was a river!"

"You remember this brook?"

"I named it the Wash, because we washed our clothes here. But I thought the Wash was a river."

"You were small then, Percy. What comes next?"

I point. "Around the bend the trail goes up a mountain. Then there's a sugar brush, and the cowshed. After that's the cabin."

"Hah! Let's see."

Johnny strides quickly ahead and disappears around the bend. I fit my pace to Peg's. I'm in no hurry to meet uncle Sol. Even so, it's exciting to see my memory prove right. Slowly we round the bend and start up the mountain. It is a pretty steep hill. I stop three times to let Peg blow and pant. Johnny is lost to sight, over the top.

All the way up through the woods yellow leaves rain down around us. Leaves land in my hair and Peg's mane. At the top the rain stops because the trees draw back. We come out into a bright, warm stillness.

Lo, to the side, the giant maples I remember! They lift bare, shining arms to the sun. The cowshed huddles at their feet, empty, door open. Cow and calf must be turned loose now in the harvested corn.

To our left, eight gnarled apple trees line the trail. I don't remember these. A ladder leans against one. A basket nestles under another. Everywhere dangle great, juicy, red apples.

Peg wants to stop and munch some windfalls. I'm glad to pause. Around the next bend we will see the cabin, Uncle Sol's cabin. My stomach flutters. If I had eaten anything I would be sick, now.

Uncle Sol is the man who fetched me away from Mama's deathbed, into the snowstorm. To the waiting Wheelers. I'm in no hurry to see him. And for sure I won't stay with him!

But as Johnny says, Uncle Sol may know of other relations. Connections with the world.

Johnny comes back eagerly, trotting around the bend. "What are you waiting for, Percy?"

"Peg likes windfalls."

"Hah!" Johnny reaches up, selects himself a fat apple. He bites it, the juice running down his sparse black beard. "I sold McKinley these trees, let's see, twelve years ago. The way the man dealt with his household, I'm surprised they grew! I'm surprised the Lord gave him a harvest! Maybe he's changed his ways." Hah! "Maybe he heard the Good News From Heaven at last, from someone else. *I haven't seen him since. But come along, now.*" Chomping his apple, Johnny hops backward toward the bend. "Come!"

We hang back. I ask, "Did you see anyone at the cabin?"

"Aye, I did."

"Did you talk to them?"

"Waited for you."

"Did you see Uncle Sol?"

"Nay, not him. Now come!" Johnny grabs Peg's lead and hauls him along, protesting.

"You're in a terrible hurry, Johnny!"

"Don't have all day! Got to get on to the blockhouse."

We round the bend.

There stands the cabin I remember, low and dark, but with a new ell to it, and new lilac bushes in the dooryard.

A rich smell of apple butter hangs in the air. Even my sick stomach answers to it joyfully! The smell comes from a kettle hung over coals in the

dooryard. A woman stands stirring the kettle. Her back is turned to us.
Johnny calls, "Hello the house!"
The woman turns.
Lo, she is chunky like me. A long braid of yellow hair like mine drapes over one shoulder. Her dress is homespun, her feet are bare. Surprise drops her mouth open, and I see two teeth missing.
Johnny advances, holding out a friendly hand.
I stare at the woman with the yellow braid and missing teeth. She stares at me.
Johnny reaches her. "Appleseed John here, M'am. Pleased to make your acquaintance."
She comes past Johnny. She starts across the yard to me.
I start across to her.
We walk into each other's arms.
Her head rests on my shoulder and mine on hers. Her heart beats against me. Her strong arms come round me, warm, as I remember them. My arms steal around her sturdy waist. The world hugs me. I hug the world.
My name is Persis McKinley. I am the small daughter... I am the big daughter of Yunis McKinley, sister of Solomon McKinley. Sol feeds us grudgingly. We work hard to be worth our cornbread. Even small brother Kevin works, best he can. Sol is hard. But Yunis is hard, too. She can stand up to winter, Indians, wolves, bears,

serpents. As long as she's got her health she can stand up to Sol McKinley. Especially now, with me beside her! The two of us together can wrap Sol McKinley right up!

"M'am," says Johnny, "Your butter's burning."

We smell it scorching. We just hug. Over Mama's shoulder I see Johnny take the paddle and stir the apple butter. We just hug.

Over Mama's shoulder I see a big boy come around the cabin with sticks for the fire. He drops them. His face lights up. He flies to Johnny. "Mr. Appleseed!"

"Ho, Kevin," says Johnny. "Your uncle to home?"

"No sir," says Kevin happily. "He's at the blockhouse. Thought you knew that, or you wouldn't be here."

"Had to come," says Johnny. "Had something for you." He nods at us. Kevin stares.

In the warm, husky voice I remember, Mama says, "I thought you was dead!"

I say, "I thought *you* was dead!"

We hug closer. We hug so close a tornado couldn't pull us apart.

Chapter 18.

UNDER JOHNNY'S APPLE TREES we say goodby.

Peg wanders nearby, searching for windfalls. At the bend in the trail golden leaves still fall like rain. Around the apple trees the sun beats down. Johnny and I pause in the shade. Johnny picks an apple and gives it to me and I bite in. It's right tart, like Johnny himself.

"I can't believe I'm saying goodby," I say.

"Well, of course we're not saying goodby," Johnny says gently. "I always come back, Percy. Always turn up, like the bad apple in the barrel."

"You promised to show me an angel, but you never did."

"Did so! You saw it in the pool. You forget because the she-bear fretted it out of your head."

"All I saw in the pool was me."

"Aye," he declares triumphantly. "You are the angel."

His eyes are deeply kind; he's not funning. "Man has a spirit, Percy, and the body is a coat for that spirit. Love God and the Neighbor, and the angel who will live forever in Heaven will be yourself. The self you saw in the pool. God bless you now, Percy McKinley."

Johnny turns to go. I grab his coffee sack. "Johnny Appleseed, I thought you wanted to marry me!"

He turns back, blue eyes wide. "*What?*" He laughs, crinkling his nose. Then, seeing my face, he sobers quickly. "Child," he says, very gentle, "I'm a loner. You grow up in a two-room cabin with ten half brothers and sisters, you'll be a loner too! I love the Neighbor dearly, but at a distance. I love space, God's air, silent woods. Silent beasts. In the great silence I hear God's voice. See?"

"But . . . if you didn't want to marry me, why did you go in among the Wyandots and buy me? You could have just gone past. Why did you bring me all this way? You could have left me at Partridges'."

" 'Good actions,' " he reminds me, " 'ought to be done because they are of God and from God and lead us to Heaven.' Speaking of which, I nearly forgot! He fishes his grungy pouch of money out and hands it to me. "Give this to Solomon McKinley for Peg's corn. I'll come back in the spring and lead him to better pasture." Once more he turns away.

But I have a gift for Johnny. Grandly, I declare, " 'The world is so full of God's love and wisdom it is an image of Him!' "

Johnny turns back. "What did you say?"

"I said, the world is an image of God because it shows His love and wisdom. Your Swedenborg told me that in a dream."

"What!"

"You said Swedenborg did nothing but write. I saw him writing in my dream. But then he went into a garden and planted seeds, and said that to me. I think, Johnny, your Swedenborg was an orchardman, like you."

Johnny gapes. I am wonderfully pleased to have given him, told him, something! I say, "I thought you'd like to know that. How else could I pay you back?"

Johnny smiles at me. "As to that, Percy, I'm well paid. Your Mama gave me three times the snuff I paid for you!"

And Johnny goes. Actually leaves. Walks away. He pauses to pat Peg's neck and feed him an apple. Then he walks away into the rain of leaves. Lo, he vanishes behind the leaves, around the bend.

But Johnny will come back. He'll come to take Peg to better pasture. He'll come to read Mama and me his Good News Straight from Heaven. He'll come because good actions are of God and from God, and lead us to Heaven.

GLOSSARY

blockhouse	a fort where settlers gathered for trade, news, and for safety
bucko time	a good time
Corn Mother	Earth Goddess of the Delaware tribe
dassn't	dare not
Delaware	Indian tribe
"eekee"	"Oh, dear" (Delaware word)
heist	lift
hominy	corn meal
hunker	squat down, one knee on the ground
in a trice	very quickly
journeycake	cornbread, also known as johnny-cake, easily carried on a journey

"makatut"	"mahkwatut," or little bear (Delaware word)
mortar	a vessel in which dried food, such as corn, is pounded with a pestle
Prophet	Tenskwatawa, brother of the Shawnee chief, Tecumseh
Seneca	one of the Iroquois nations, native to western Pennsylvania and southwest New York
slavey	underpaid, overworked servant
Tecumseh	Shawnee chief who tried to unite several tribes to drive settlers out of Indian lands. He fought for the British and was killed in the War of 1812.
Wyandot	Indian tribe

ABOUT JOHNNY APPLESEED

JOHN CHAPMAN (JOHNNY APPLESEED) was born September 26, 1774 in Leominster, Massachusetts. His mother, Elizabeth Simons Chapman, died in 1776.

His father, Nathaniel Chapman, a Revolutionary Minute Man, married again and raised a second family of ten children. In his teens John left home and became a woods traveler, a planter and seller of apple trees, and later a Swedenborgian missionary.

He traveled and planted in Pennsylvania, Ohio, and Indiana, making friends of settlers and Indians alike. In 1812 (when he was thirty-eight) John warned settlers of Indian attacks. He also rescued a girl from her Indian captors and brought her home through the wilderness.

The adventures recounted in this story are elements of John Chapman's legend. He was kind to all and friendly with wild animals. He lived according to his own and Swedenborg's teachings.

John Chapman died in March, 1845 in the cabin of his friends, Mr. and Mrs. William Worth. On his way to tend one of his orchards he fell sick and "in a day or two . . . he passed to the spirit land."

His monument declares, HE LIVED FOR OTHERS.

His legend lives on.

ABOUT EMANUEL SWEDENBORG

EMANUEL SWEDENBORG WAS BORN January 29, 1688 in Stockholm, Sweden, to Sarah Behm Swedberg and Jesper Swedberg. When Jesper became Bishop of Skara, the family was ennobled and the name changed to Swedenborg.

When Emanuel was eight his mother died. He was raised by his stepmother, sister, and relatives. He never married.

A brilliant student, Emanuel learned Latin and Greek, mathematics, and philosophy. He traveled to England and Europe, studying astronomy, bookbinding, watchmaking, engraving, and lens-grinding. He published Sweden's first scientific journal with articles about some of his inventions.

Swedenborg was appointed to the Board of Mines. Mining is still a major industry in Sweden.

As a member of the House of Nobles, Swedenborg proposed legislation on the economy and peace.

As a scientist, Swedenborg continued to investigate all the fields of science then known. His studies led to the new sciences of crystallography and metallurgy. Many of his ideas were far ahead of their time, such as his theories about the formation of the solar system and the structure of the atom. Swedenborg became interested in human anatomy, and in the brain. While researching the brain, he began to experience strange dreams. Swedenborg meditated in order to understand his own mind.

In 1745, Swedenborg began to experience wonderful visions about the world within the mind. His life changed completely. The scientist spent the rest of life writing about spiritual realities.

Swedenborg wrote that God is One and has revealed himself to man. Man's purpose in this life is to grow in love and service. God does not judge man and assign him to heaven or to hell; rather, it is the life which is led on earth that leads a soul to choose where the afterlife will be spent. We are all angels (or devils) right now on earth. But we have the freedom to change and grow in this lifetime.

Swedenborg once promised a young girl that he would show her an angel. She sat down in front of a curtain and closed her eyes. Swedenborg drew the curtain aside, and when she looked up, there was a mirror with her own reflection.

In his own life, Swedenborg used his talents to

serve humanity and showed kindness and cheerful courtesy wherever he went.

Swedenborg died in London on March 29, 1772, as he himself had prophesied.

QUOTES FROM EMANUEL SWEDENBORG

The interior memory vastly excels the exterior.

The Lord guards man with most especial care during his sleep.

It is plain that as each and all things in the world have come forth from the Divine, they continue to come forth from the Divine.

The whole Heaven is full of uses, so that it ought to be called the kingdom of uses.

All things in the world exist from a Divine origin. All God's creatures have spiritual correspondences and uses.

Among the Gentiles in Heaven the most beloved are the Africans. They accept the good and true elements of Heaven more readily than others.

A man is as the quality of his love is. If there be with a man the love of God and the love of the Neighbor he is, as to his spirit which lives on after death, an angel; no matter how he appears in the external world.

There is but one life which is the Lord's, and this life flows in and causes man to live. All those throughout the world who have lived in good are, of the Lord's mercy, received and saved.

Man . . . becomes a true likeness of Heaven to the extent that he is involved in the good of love and faith.

The person who possesses what is good from the Lord is an angel-man.

Good actions ought to be done because they are of God and from God, and lead us to Heaven.

So full of Divine Love and Divine Wisdom is the universe in greatest and least, in first and last things, that it may be said to be Divine Love and Divine Wisdom in an image.